POKÉMON

THE MOVIE

MEWTWO RETURNS

There are more books
about Pokémon.

Collect them all!

POKéMON
THE MOVIE
MEWTWO RETURNS

Adaptation by Howie Dewin
Based on the Pokémon Home Video
screenplay by Michael Haigney

SCHOLASTIC INC.
New York   Toronto   London   Auckland   Sydney
Mexico City   New Delhi   Hong Kong
Buenos Aires

ISBN 0-439-38564-4

12 11 10 9 8 7 6 5 4 3 2 1   2 3 4 5 6/0

Printed in the U.S.A.
First Scholastic printing, January 2002

JOHTO REGION

Contents

Mewtwo Remembers

Not so long ago, in a secret laboratory on a remote island, a team of determined scientists created the very first Pokémon clone. The scientists had discovered the fossilized remains of Mew, an ancient and legendary Pokémon. But it was Giovanni, leader of the evil Team Rocket, who ordered the scientists to use that fossil to create the world's most powerful Pokémon.

The scientists filled their laboratories with large glass tanks that bubbled with red fluid. Inside one of the tanks was a muscular Pokémon with sleek white fur. It had big eyes and a long tail. It looked like a very large version of Mew. It floated lifeless in the tank for a long time.

Then, one day, it opened its big eyes. Mewtwo was alive and angry! It wanted to be more than an experiment. So the muscular Pokémon used its psychic powers. It shattered its tank and destroyed the laboratory.

Giovanni convinced Mewtwo to work with him. He trained the Pokémon to control its abilities. But Mewtwo soon realized Giovanni was no different than the scientists. He considered Mewtwo his personal property.

Mewtwo knew it was more than an experiment even though it had been created in a lab rather than born. It was still alive. It had been used and betrayed by its creators. Mewtwo felt completely alone and wanted revenge.

Mewtwo lured some of the world's best Pokémon trainers to its island fortress and seized their Pokémon. Then it made copies of them, as it had been cloned from Mew.

But soon, Mewtwo encountered its nemesis, Mew. There was a great battle to decide who would rule — Pokémon born into this world or the cloned Pokémon created by Mewtwo. Just as Mew and Mewtwo were preparing for a final confrontation that may have destroyed them all, a young trainer cried out for the fighting to cease — Ash Ketchum.

Ash's selfless actions puzzled Mewtwo. It could not understand a human who valued *all* Pokémon, whether born or created. The battle ceased and when Mewtwo opened its eyes, it also opened its heart.

Mewtwo and the clones left to find a place where they could live in peace — away from humans. Mewtwo wiped out all memories of the struggle with its psychic powers. Now, no one remembers Mewtwo except for the one who created it. For Giovanni, the desire to control the world's most powerful Pokémon still burns.

Lost and Found

The image on the big screen looked like a moonscape. A young girl pointed to the image as she talked to a large man who stared at the screen. They were alone at the Team Rocket headquarters.

"These are live satellite pictures of a remote area of the Johto Region, Giovanni," said the girl. "Extreme weather makes it un-inhabitable . . . for people." Giovanni studied the image. His Pokémon, Persian, studied him. "But keep watching," the girl added. The camera zoomed in on an unusual shape. Giovanni smiled.

"I've found you," he said in a low, threatening voice.

The image was fuzzy but it was clear enough. It was Mewtwo.

Mewtwo stood at the edge of a rocky cliff deep in the Johto Region. The ocean spread out before it. Behind Mewtwo, the Pokémon clones watched the sky fill with the colors of the dawn.

"This place is . . . beautiful," Mewtwo's voice was deep and commanding. "But what right have I to judge? We . . . are clones . . . copies . . . products of science. We are outcasts. We must live as outcasts . . . if we are to live at all. We shall stay here . . . far from the world . . . far from man. It is our only hope. For if we do not live in secret, we shall never live in peace."

At the same time, Ash Ketchum found himself in the Johto region, too. His friends Misty and Brock were with him along with Misty's Pokémon, Togepi, and of course, Ash's

Pikachu. They were all about to come upon an amazing sight. Ash had experienced a lot of amazing things since he began his journey as a Pokémon trainer on his tenth birthday. Two of the best things were meeting Misty and Pokémon gym leader, Brock. But the very best thing was getting Pikachu, his loyal Electric Pokémon.

The trio suddenly stopped walking. Ash's mouth fell open. The most majestic canyon and lush valley he'd ever seen lay before him.

"That must be . . . !" exclaimed Misty.

"Must be!" agreed Ash.

Brock came up behind them, "That's it all right . . . Purity Canyon — the Johto Region's greatest natural wonder."

"No wonder!" said Ash. He'd never seen such enormous cliffs.

"Wonder how we get across it?" Misty asked.

"The book says it's almost impossible by foot," said Brock. "The only way to get across is by bus, but it only makes the trip once a month."

"When does it leave?" Misty asked.

"Lunchtime today," answered Brock.

"That must be the bus down there!" squealed Misty.

"C'mon!" shouted Ash. "Maybe we can catch it."

"Pika!" exclaimed the little yellow Poké-mon from its perch on Ash's shoulder.

As the friends raced down the danger-ous slope of the canyon, the skies darkened. It began to rain. The path became very slip-pery.

Although they didn't know it, Ash and his friends were being watched. The sneaky Team Rocket, Jessie, James, and Meowth, had followed them to the Johto region. Once again, they were determined to steal Ash's Pikachu. They just needed the right oppor-tunity. Jessie watched Ash, Misty, Brock, and their Pokémon through a set of binoc-ulars.

"Look at those twerps running in the rain," she hissed.

"It's a good thing I packed this um-brella!" James crowed.

Meowth, a rare English-speaking Poké-mon, looked up from a guidebook. "Yeah, but what are we going to do when the bad weather hits?"

"This *is* bad weather! What are you talking about?" Jessie snapped at Meowth.

"I'm talkin' about typhoons."

Jessie and James were shocked. "Typhoons?"

Meowth's reading was drowned out by the noise of the terrible winds. They clung to the umbrella pole. But the wind was too strong.

"How many times must our plans be destroyed!" shouted Jessie.

"Before they're allowed to be tried?" finished James.

Just before the wind carried them away, they shouted, "We're blasting off again!"

Ash, Misty, and Brock were not in much better shape. They were moments away from the bus stop. But it didn't matter. Luna, the bus dispatcher, had just given the driver permission to leave early to avoid the weather.

"Hey! Wait for us!" yelled Ash. Just then,

Brock lost his footing. He tumbled into Misty. She and Togepi went flying onto Ash and Pikachu. They careened down the canyon trail in a tangled mess. They landed at the feet of Luna.

"Are you okay?" asked Luna from under her bright pink raincoat.

"Do you know if the bus to Purity Canyon stops here?" Ash asked.

"Yes, but you just missed it," she answered.

"There's got to be a way to catch that bus!" Ash demanded.

Luna smiled. "Not when the weather gets like this! The wind and the rain are treacherous here, and the roads can become incredibly *dangerous*. It's hard enough to make it by bus. On foot you don't have a chance!"

Ash didn't want to believe Luna but the weather was only getting worse.

Luna pointed to a log cabin lodge. "Why don't we all get out of this rain?"

They followed her inside. Down the road, the bus slipped and slid. It was spinning out of control in the wind and rain.

Then a sudden gust actually lifted it into the air. The passengers screamed. They were going to crash! There was no doubt about it.

But they didn't crash. Somehow, they were delivered gently back to the ground. It was as if a giant hand had reached down and saved them. Luka, the bus driver, couldn't understand it.

"How could this happen?" she whispered.

Nobody had an answer.

Chapter Two

Across the Valley

Deep within the mountain rock, Mewtwo stood in its headquarters with two Pokémon clones. They studied a large projection screen. It showed the bus floating safely back to the ground. Pikachu X and Meowth X were confused.

"You ask . . . why did I save those humans?" Mewtwo said quietly.

Pikachu X nodded.

"For our own protection," answered Mewtwo. "An accident would bring human rescuers. We might be discovered . . . and our peace disrupted."

"*Meowth!*" Meowth X challenged.

Mewtwo sat on his rock throne. "You believe there is another reason? That I felt concern? That I cared about the safety of those humans? I assure you, that was not the case. I could never feel compassion for humans."

Meanwhile, Ash, Misty, and Brock still needed to cross the valley.

"People who miss the bus stay here until the next one comes around in a month," said Luna. She gestured to the comfortable, cozy living room of the wooden lodge.

"We can't stay here a whole month!" cried Ash. "Isn't there any other way?"

"Well, you could take a boat down Purity River at the base of the canyon and get across the valley *that* way," replied Luna as she sipped a hot cup of tea.

At the mention of water, Misty lit up. "I'd *love* to take a boat ride. My family runs a Water Pokémon gym. I just *love* the water!"

Luna smiled. "If you love water, you

have come to the right place!" She led them out to the deck. Above them was huge magnificent waterfall. Below them, there was a beautiful pool of water.

Luna lowered a bucket into the pool. It filled with water so clear it sparkled.

"Have a drink, Brock!" She offered him a cup.

Brock took a long gulp. His knees nearly buckled. "This water is absolutely *delicious*!" he exclaimed.

"Hey *I* wanna try some, *too*!" insisted Misty.

She took one gulp and was starry-eyed. "It makes me feel refreshingly alive and tingly!"

Ash, Pikachu, and Togepi tried the water, too. It was clearly extraordinary.

Misty said, "I can hardly wait to ride on a river that's this super-pure and clean. Come on, guys! Let's go!"

The three friends paddled their way through a stunning landscape. The plants were lush. The water was completely clear all the way to the bottom of the river.

"I'm kind of glad we missed the bus, Brock. The current is doing most of the work and the water's crystal clear!" Misty said.

Brock smiled. "I wouldn't be so happy about this nice clean water if I were you. I know how much you hate Bug Pokémon," he said. "Nice clean water is just what Bug Pokémon love."

Misty looked around. "I'm not going to let them bug me!" she declared.

They paddled past huge green trees with thick vines. In the distance, Ash saw something glittering like a Christmas tree.

"That's a flock of Ledian. They're Bug Pokémon. They glow like that on clear, starry nights."

Misty smiled. She tried to convince herself she was starting to like Bug Pokémon. But her breath quickened as hundreds of hard cocoonlike shells appeared above her head.

"I wouldn't be surprised to see a bunch of Beedrill, too," said Brock. "With this many Kakuna here there's gotta be some around."

Suddenly, it seemed to Misty like Bug Pokémon were everywhere. She couldn't take it! She turned the canoe around and paddled them back to the lodge in a fury.

"You should have mentioned you don't like Bug Pokémon," Luna said.

"Is there any other way across the valley?" Ash asked impatiently. He studied the terrain from the lodge deck.

"We can go straight over the top of Mt. Quena!" announced Brock. The mountain was so high, Ash could barely see the top.

"I don't think you want to take that route," Luna warned. "Mt. Quena is the highest mountain in the whole Johto Region. At the top of the mountain is Clarity Lake. It goes on for miles and miles and the water is incredibly clean and clear. It's beautiful, but humans could never live there. The height of the mountain and the weather even keep visitors away. The only ones that live up there are some wild Pokémon — types that can thrive in the extreme conditions."

Ash perked up. "If there are Pokémon up there, I say we go!" he exclaimed.

Just then, strange music floated through the air.

"*Pika?*" said Pikachu.

Togepi looked up at the sky.

"It's a flock of Butterfree!" cried Ash.

The sky filled with the beautiful Pokémon. They sailed gracefully past the huge harvest moon.

In another part of the valley, Mewtwo watched the Buttefree sadly. He turned to Pikachu X and Meowth X.

"For these Pokémon . . . life is as it should be. They were born into this world. It is their home. . . . they belong here. But where do we belong?"

Up, Up, and Away

Bang! Bang! Everyone on Luna's deck spun around in surprise.

"Good morning!" they heard from the other side of the door.

"Hello?" replied Luna. She was surprised. Guests didn't usually arrive so late. She opened the door.

"I said 'good morning,'" piped the cheery blond girl with pigtails, "because even though it's after midnight, if I said 'good night' you might go to bed!" She stood next to a handsome dark-haired young man with big brown eyes. They entered the lodge. Luna, Ash, and his pals were too stunned to say anything.

"We hate to bother you," said the young man, "but we've been doing some exploring and we need a place to spend the night. My name is Cullen Calix."

"I know that name," Luna said, "you're the famous researcher and Professor of medicine."

Cullen smiled and nodded. He replied, "and if my guess is right you're Luna Carson. I've read dozens of your research papers on Pokémon."

Luna welcomed the pair into the lodge. She saw the confusion on Ash's face.

"Working for the bus company is my part-time job. I'm actually here observing native Pokémon and their habitats."

The blond-haired girl gasped. "I can't believe I'm meeting *the* Luna Carson. I'm, like, a total fan of yours!"

Luna smiled slightly. "And you are?"

"This is Domino. She works for the Pokémon Institute," answered Cullen.

Domino giggled and waved.

"I'm afraid the bus won't be back for another month," Luna told them.

"Oh, I came to study the water," replied Cullen. "I've been studying the Purity River for some time, and I've discovered that its water contains a number of rare minerals that have an amazing effect on the health of both Pokémon and human volunteers. I've come to explore Mt. Quena and unravel the secret." Cullen was obviously delighted to share his great news. But Luna was not so pleased.

"That's too bad," she said. "If the water does heal people, they'll come here from all over. They might accidentally destroy the very thing they're looking for."

"I see what you mean," Cullin said, suddenly concerned. But the noise of exploding firecrackers stopped the conversation.

"Team Rocket blasting off at the speed of light!" exclaimed Jessie as she sprang onto the deck.

"Surrender now or prepare to fight, fight, fight!" James added.

"*Meowth*, that's right!" declared the scratch-cat Pokémon.

Ash, Misty, and Brock shook their heads in disgust. "What do you want?" they demanded. Team Rocket always showed up at the most inconvenient moments. But even worse, they always tried to steal Pikachu.

"Today's the day we capture Pikachu!" announced Jessie.

"Never!" shouted Ash.

"*Pika!*" the Pokémon spat back. Misty and Brock were ready to defend Pikachu and so were Luna and Cullen. Domino, however, seemed more interested in Team Rocket. She looked at them in disgust.

"Go electricity absorbing wire!" shouted James. Instantly, a coiled-up wire shot out and grabbed Pikachu. The little yellow Pokémon was wrapped up in the wire before Ash could say a word. Pikachu tried to shock James but the wire absorbed all the voltage. Team Rocket just laughed. They held on to Pikachu and climbed aboard their huge Meowth-headed balloon.

"It's time for our getaway!" Meowth said.

"We've burst that thing before. We'll do it again!" declared Ash.

Ash, Pikachu, and their friends set out for
a new adventure in the Johto Region.

Luna and Cullen
are ready for
action.

They'll take on
Team Rocket if
they have to!

"You cannot conquer me!"

Mewtwo and Giovanni face off.

Giovanni wants to create an army of the world's most powerful Pokémon — and rule the Earth!

Mewtwo will never give in and join Team
Rocket . . . unless it's the only way to save
its Pokémon friends from destruction.

Mewtwo and its
friends try to
escape from
Giovanni's forces.

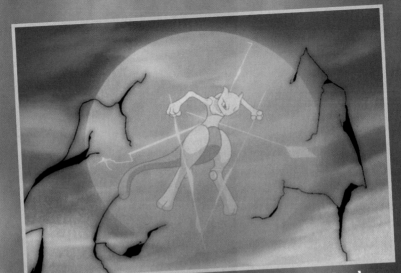

Giovanni takes control of Mewtwo's body. But will he gain control of Mewtwo's mind?

Ash, Pikachu, and their friends charge into action to rescue Mewtwo.

The water in the spring might save
Mewtwo. If Giovanni and the Team Rocket
troops would just get out of the way!

Mewtwo spots Mew while in
the spring's healing waters.

Mewtwo emerges — stronger than ever!
And ready to take on its toughest foe.

Together, Mewtwo and Ash
have defeated Giovanni.
The Earth is safe — for now!

"Not anymore," teased Jessie. "We've always had the team but now we've finally got the rocket!" The balloon powered up its new rockets.

Quietly, Domino said, "They're embarrassing!" The rocket boosters launched and the balloon went barreling upward.

"Pikachu!" shouted Ash. It was too late.

"The weather is changing," Luna declared as she watched from the deck. "Taking off in a balloon is careless and reckless."

"I have to follow Team Rocket, no matter what!" Ash cried.

Luna gathered up her mountain climbing gear and said, "I know Mt. Quena pretty well. I'll lead you up there!"

In a matter of minutes, the whole crew was climbing up the dangerous mountain.

"This is so scary," whined Domino.

"You should've stayed at the lodge," scolded Cullen.

"That would have been even scarier," she giggled.

The wind picked up. The climbing got more difficult. Luna led the way as they pulled themselves up the mountain along a long rope. The wind was giving Team Rocket a tough time, too.

"We're not getting anywhere," snipped James. Just then, a terrible wind pulled them across the sky. They flew right by Ash and the others.

"There goes Team Rocket!" shouted Ash. "Hey, come back here!" The balloon was out of control. The wind pulled it closer and closer to the moutain and the hikers.

"Look out! It's heading right this way!" Luna shouted just as the balloon collided with the mountain climbers. The mountain-climbing rope snagged on the balloon basket. The rope pulled away from the rock. Ash and all his friends were hanging in midair!

As they hung on for dear life, a gigantic lake and island came into view. Domino secretly pulled out a pair of binoculars. She inspected the island.

"I think I see just what we're looking for," she said. She flashed a devious smile.

Chapter Four

Pikachu vs. Pikachu

Ash and his friends clung to the rope. Mewtwo watched them on a monitor in its headquarters. "Those children again," it murmured to itself. Mewtwo stared at the screen but didn't see Domino as she pulled out a two-way radio.

"It's definitely Mewtwo," she said into the radio. On the other side of the transmission, Giovanni smiled.

"You got away from me once," he sneered. "It won't happen again. Double-oh-nine, begin operations at once," Giovanni commanded.

"Copy! Over and out!" Domino flew into action. She raced up the rope. She climbed over Ash and Luna and everyone else in her way. Before anyone could figure out what was happening, Domino was in the balloon basket.

"Hey!" cried Jessie. "Who are you?"

Domino didn't bother responding. She pulled out her radio and spoke. "Double-oh-nine to Team Rocket Combat Unit leaders. Proceed to coordinates."

"The Team Rocket Combat Unit?" James was in disbelief.

"They're here?" Jessie couldn't believe their luck. She looked across the sky and saw a fleet of yellow blimplike balloons rising up from the horizon.

"Impressive," James uttered.

Just then, Ash pulled himself up into the basket. "Now we got you!" he gasped. By the time Misty, Brock, and Cullen appeared, Ash realized something very strange was going on.

"Domino, what are you doing?" Cullen demanded.

Domino didn't speak. She spun herself into a blur and was suddenly wearing boots, a miniskirt, and a shirt with the unmistakable "R" for Team Rocket. "My fellow agents know me as double-oh-nine, but my adversaries know me simply as the Black Tulip."

She laughed. Her violet eyes darted back and forth under her white cap. She pulled out a jet-black tulip with a dangerously sharp stem. She jumped up on the edge of the basket. "Here's a little souvenir!" she cackled. The tulip stem went sailing up into the balloon. A huge rip appeared. The balloon screeched sideways and plummeted.

"Bye! Nice to see you go!" Domino laughed. She pulled out a compact hang glider and took off toward the island. Behind her, terrified screams filled the night sky.

Jessie, James, and Meowth covered their faces and didn't look up until everything stopped moving. They found themselves hanging from a tree branch. The balloon ropes had tangled in the branches.

"Well," muttered James, "at least we finally captured the twerp's Pikachu. That's progress!" Then he realized Pikachu was no longer wrapped in the electric cord.

"It must have gotten loose when the balloon crashed," said Meowth. It pointed to Pikachu. The Electric Pokémon was down on the ground looking up at Team Rocket. Little sparks shot off the Pokémon.

"Why is it sparking like that?" James asked.

ZAP! Pikachu didn't leave time for an answer. Team Rocket was shaken to the rocky ground by the force of the Pikachu's electricity.

"It went easy on us that time," Jessie managed to groan. "I wonder why."

The trio shook off the shock and looked back at Pikachu. But what they saw was more than shocking. Pikachu was staring up to a rock plateau where Pikachu X sat. The two Pokémon didn't seem pleased to see each other.

"What're they saying, Meowth?" Jessie demanded.

Meowth listened carefully. "That one up there said, 'So, we meet again.'"

"They know each other?" James was confused.

"The one on the hill sure knows the twerp's Pikachu," answered Meowth. "It ain't happy. It's sayin', 'You shouldn't have come here. This place is ours!'"

"*Pika-pika-chu!*" Pikachu X's tone was angry.

Meowth continued, "It said, 'We came here to make a new home and live in peace but you brought humans! That's the last thing Pokémon clones need!'"

"*Pika?*" Ash's Pikachu seemed as confused as Team Rocket.

"'Get out or you'll regret it!'" Meowth interpreted. Pikachu X came down the plateau.

"Looks like they're about to battle!" James said excitedly.

Jessie squealed. "Pikachu vs. Pikachu? This could be the match of the year!"

Ash's Pikachu was not excited. The last thing it wanted was to battle its copy.

Chapter Five

Mewtwo Decides

Mewtwo's psychic powers stopped the action in midair. Pikachu X was hurling toward Pikachu when Mewtwo overpowered it.

"Fighting is senseless," the Psychic Pokémon said ⸱ quietly to the Pokémon clones gathered around. "There is nothing to be gained from such battling. You are the same as other Pokémon, neither stronger nor weaker. You proved that the last time we met and battled the Pokémon from which we were copied."

"This is awfully confusing," whispered Jessie.

Pikachu X floated to the ground. Mewtwo released the Electric Pokémon from its psychic grip.

"I've searched for a place to live in secret and in peace," Mewtwo continued. "Now these humans have found us again. Perhaps we shall never find peace."

Pikachu X sparked angrily.

"It's saying their only choice is to stand their ground," Meowth spoke aloud. "If they don't, their home will get taken away from them. They gotta battle!"

A roar of support rose up from the Pokémon gathered, including Gyarados, Vaporeon, and Blastoise. Meowth looked around nervously.

"*Pika-pi!*" pleaded Ash's Pikachu.

"Pikachu's right," agreed Meowth. "There's no reason for you Pokémon to fight us Pokémon!"

"We are shadows," Mewtwo said. "We must live in the shadows of moonlight."

Pikachu X sparked.

"It's sayin' it ain't fair that they have to live like shadows," Meowth said. "This place is beautiful. But beyond this place there's a big wide world."

Pikachu X was beginning to spark with serious anger again. It wanted to be able to live in that "big wide world."

"'You know that world, don't you Pikachu?'" Meowth translated. "'You were born in it and you can live in it. But we can't! Whatever we do or wherever we go, we don't belong.'"

As Jessie listened to the sad tale of the Pokémon clones, she got very upset. "I know that feeling. Ever since I was a little girl, the world has always treated me as someone who doesn't really belong."

"Enough," demanded Mewtwo. "We are what we are. We will remain here and live in peace . . . if we can."

Jessie, James, and Meowth watched as the Pokémon stood quietly in the moonlight. For the moment, they seemed peaceful.

What they didn't know was that Giovanni was monitoring them from his helicopter. The Team Rocket Combat Unit was not far behind.

"Prepare, my old friend," he hissed at the image of Mewtwo. "For at sunrise, we will meet again."

Chapter Six

Straight to the Source

"Is everybody okay?" Brock asked.

They were all still in the water where they had crash-landed. They were surrounded by forest.

"I'm all right," answered Misty.

Togepi agreed.

"I won't be fine until I see Pikachu again," said Ash.

"Team Rocket's balloon was headed for that island, Ash," Cullen said.

Ash immediately started walking toward the island.

"Ash wait!" Luna exclaimed. "See that giant tree trunk? We'll build a canoe out of it."

"We can use our Pokémon to help!" Misty added.

Ash wasted no time. "Chikorita! Bulbasaur! I choose you!"

The two Pokémon flew toward the log. They shot sharp-edged leaves at the wood. The bladelike foliage carved away at the wood. A canoe began to emerge. Before long, the gang was rowing toward the island.

Back on the island, Meowth was still translating for Jessie and James.

"The other Pikachu said, 'If we don't do something to get out of here, they're going to catch us and use us in Pokémon cloning experiments.'"

The clone Pokémon rumbled in agreement.

"I say we leave this place and go where we please!" Meowth spoke for Pikachu X.

"Ask them to bring us, too!" James begged Meowth.

"We'll go anywhere!" Jessie agreed.

The Pokémon took Jessie and James at their word. They threw the nasty pair into a jail cell.

"You're on Team Rocket," Jessie snipped at Meowth. "Why aren't you locked up?"

"I'm valuable because I talk human talk," Meowth gloated. Then he turned and headed off with Ash's Pikachu and the clones.

High above the water, Mewtwo watched the Pokémon clones. They were traveling across the water to escape the island.

"Should I let them go?" Mewtwo asked itself. "Here I can use my powers to protect them from harm. But do I have the right to keep them from living as they choose?"

Ash's canoe entered a grotto on the island. When they were well inside the cave, Ash jumped from the canoe. He dashed toward a long flight of stone stairs that led up from the water. He had to find Pikachu. When he reached the top, he stopped in his tracks. A stunning lake spread out before him.

"What is this place?" he asked.

Cullen gasped. He immediately took a

water sample. "Wow! Luna, this spring must be the source for Purity River. The water's chemical makeup is astounding!"

"This place is bursting with life," Luna pointed out. She gestured to the lush green growth. There were beautiful flowers and fruit hanging from the trees. "That's because it's clean here, untouched, pure. The source of that purity is the spring."

"This spring could be the way to bring health and happiness to the whole world!" Cullen exclaimed.

"Oh, cuties!" cried Misty. A group of young Nidoqueen and Rhyhorn were passing in front of her.

"Wow," said Brock. "Without a Pokémon breeder, it's amazing they look so healthy."

"In a habitat as clean as this one they couldn't help but grow up to be strong and healthy," Luna explained.

Ash looked around at the happy, healthy Pokémon. He saw their proud, protective parents watching over them from above. He could only think of Pikachu.

"I just hope Pikachu is someplace nice and safe," was all he could say.

Clone vs. Machine

"I made it!" Meowth exclaimed.

Gyarados, Wigglytuff, Ninetales, Pidgeot, and the other runaway clones pulled themselves from the water. They had made it to the mainland. But there was no time to celebrate. Team Rocket's Combat Unit rose up from nowhere. The terrified Pokémon had nowhere to run. A trapdoor opened on the underbelly of Giovanni's chopper and a laser gun appeared. It fired strange balls of red light. The balls stunned the Pokémon as soon as they were hit. First, Gyarados was struck. Then, Wigglytuff and Ninetales went down. All along the shore, clone Pokémon were attacked as they tried to flee. Another door opened on the chopper and Poké Balls fired down. Each ball consumed one of the helpless Pokémon.

Then, a red ball hurled through the sky toward Pikachu and Pikachu X. Together, they blasted the red ball with an electric jolt. They were saved. But Giovanni was not giving up. He fired again. The Pikachu ran for their lives.

Meowth hurried to Meowth X. It was stunned and laying still on the ground.

"Come on! Hurry! Pull yourself together!" Meowth carried Meowth X away before it could be captured in a Poke Ball.

Giovanni fired another round of energy balls at the Pikachu. His aim was perfect. There was nowhere to run. The Pikachu braced themselves for the blast. But nothing happened.

Pikachu looked up. Mewtwo floated above. It was throwing its own kind of energy ball, stronger than Giovanni's. Then,

Mewtwo gathered the Poké Balls that lay along the shore. One by one, it hurled them through the air freeing the captured clones. Wigglytuff exploded from the first ball. Blastoise roared out of the next. As Vaporeon reappeared, Giovanni's chopper dropped down in the sky. It hovered alongside Mewtwo.

"You," the Psychic Pokémon said.

Giovanni stepped onto the deck. Domino and Persian stood beside him.

"It's been quite a while," Giovanni sneered. "You look well."

"Leave this place at once," Mewtwo demanded. "I warn you. My strength is far greater than when we first met."

"That comes as no surprise," Giovanni replied. "My technicians predicted it and created new technology to deal with it."

Two weapens floated up from the chopper. One blue orb and one red orb rotated into position. Laser guns emerged from the orbs and were aimed at Mewtwo. In a split second, both weapons fired. Mewtwo fell to the ground. But Giovanni had no time to gloat. A second later, Mewtwo rose.

"You cannot conquer me," Mewtwo uttered.

"Your psychic attacks bend the wills of living creatures but they cannot influence machines," said Giovanni smugly.

"We will see," Mewtwo retorted.

Giovanni's weapons circled Mewtwo. Domino threw a switch on the control panel. Mewtwo was blasted with an energy field from both sides. It struggled against the machines. It focused its psychic power on both machines. Mewtwo was stronger. The machines slammed into the rock of the mountain. They appeared to be destroyed.

"Well done, Mewtwo," Giovanni oozed.

"Do not test of the limits of my power," Mewtwo warned.

"It appears that would be futile," Giovanni replied. "So we'll take our battle over to that island." He chuckled. Mewtwo looked toward the island that had become their home. It was filled with Pokémon clones that needed protection.

"I'll fly over for Phase Two," announced

Domino. Using a jet pack, she led Team Rocket to the island.

"Now we'll see how powerful your loyalties are," Giovanni hissed at Mewtwo.

"You're despicable," the Pokémon replied.

On the island, Ash, Luna, Cullen, and Misty heard the rumble of the approaching attack.

"What's going on?" Misty cried.

Whap! Whap! Whap! Ash, Luna, and Cullen felt something tightening around their middles. They looked down to see small metal clamps.

"Unfortunately, your being here is very inconvenient for us," announced Domino. She stood with an army behind her. "We can't let anyone interfere and prevent us from reaching our objectives," she continued. "We can't let you leave until our operation is over."

Ash struggled to escape. "You better!" he cried. How would Ash ever find Pikachu if he was a prisoner?

Mewtwo Submits

The next morning, Ash, Luna, Misty, and Cullen were still prisoners. Domino was proving to be every bit as mean-spirited as Giovanni.

"Aren't they simply adorable," she cooed as a group of three young Rhyhorn crossed her path. The parents of the young Poké-mon watched from above.

"Those Pokémon are just babies," cried Luna. "Leave them alone!"

Domino chuckled. She planned to cap-ture the young Pokémon. The Rhyhorn parents swooped down to protect their young. But Domino pulled out a black tulip.

"I know trainers catch their Pokémon with Poké Balls, but I prefer our method!" She fired the tulip into the ground. It acted like a high-voltage wire. It knocked out all the Pokémon. The Nidoqueen and Rhyhorn fell first. But Domino didn't stop. She stunned a Squirtle, a Psyduck, an Eevee, and many others. They littered the ground.

"These Pokémon are just going to be used in experiments and bait for Mewtwo," said Domino coldly. "No sense in wasting Poké Balls." She commanded her evil troops to gather the Pokémon. There was nothing Ash and his friends could do.

"Double-oh-nine to Giovanni," Domino spoke into her radio. "Except for the Pokémon brought by a young trainer, the island is populated by Pokémon clones . . . and we've got them! Over."

Giovanni responded from his chopper. It hovered between the island and the mainland. "Excellent," he said. "The trap is set and now we have the bait. Mewtwo, are you going to let your little friends battle me alone?"

On the ground, the Psychic Pokémon answered Giovanni. "I cannot. I must help them."

The runaway clones stood with Mewtwo. They let out a rumble.

"These guys want to help, too!" shouted Meowth.

"*Pika-Pika-pi*," Pikachu agreed.

Mewtwo accepted their offer. "Friends," he announced, "to the island!"

The gang of Pokémon took to the air. Giovanni let out another evil laugh. He alerted Domino. Mewtwo was on its way.

Mewtwo and the Pokémon came into view.

"I've been expecting you," Domino sneered. She held one of the young Nido-queen firmly.

"Release that young one," Mewtwo commanded.

"Maybe you should take that up with my boss," Domino said. Giovanni's chopper appeared. Giovanni and Persian stood on the deck.

"If you defy me, your fellow 'creations' will all be used in our experiments!" Giovanni shouted.

Mewtwo was enraged. But it couldn't betray the other clones. "Stand away!" it demanded of the Pokémon. "I must submit to him."

The red and blue orb-shaped machines reappeared. They floated down to the ground and then each shot a bolt of electricity into the sky. When the two bolts touched, a blue energy field appeared.

"This is not meant to destroy you," Giovanni said. "It has been developed to simply harness your ability and mold your will to my purposes."

"If you try to fight us, your little friends will be the ones to pay the price!" hissed Domino. To prove her point, she shot a ball of energy from the bulb of the tulip. It slammed into Pikachu. The Pokémon sailed backward. Pikachu X rushed to its side, but Domino sent out a second attack. Now both

Pikachu were struck unconscious. Mewtwo could watch no more.

"I will do as you say!" it shouted. It walked toward the blue light.

The Pokémon cried out for Mewtwo to stop. But Mewtwo was determined not to let any more Pokémon suffer.

"That's a good Pokémon," said Giovanni smugly. "You won't run away again."

"You may control my body but you will never control my will!" Mewtwo said.

The great Pokémon stepped into the light. The orb turned pink as it battled to control Mewtwo. Mewtwo winced in pain.

"We'll see," responded Giovanni.

"I will not submit," choked Mewtwo. It trembled, fighting for its will.

"You are strong, Mewtwo. But pain makes the body master of the will. Let's see how long they struggle."

Mewtwo's moans filled the air. The other Pokémon watched in horror. Giovanni surveyed the beautiful island. "This is a very charming place," he chuckled. "It's perfect for my new laboratory. I will create a vast

army of the world's most powerful Pokémon! And you," he spoke to Mewtwo, "will
be at its head carrying out my commands!"

Mewtwo could not respond. The energy
field was zapping it of all its power. Its cry
was all that could be heard.

Chapter Nine

Bug Pokémon Revenge

Ash couldn't hear Mewtwo's cries. He was being marched through cave after cave by Domino and the Team Rocket soldiers. He had no idea how he would ever save Pikachu now. But then, suddenly, the Electric Pokémon and its clone appeared. They were prisoners, too.

"Pikachu!" exclaimed Ash. "You both look wiped out! What'd they do to you?"

"Luna!" Cullen cried. "Get the spring water. It may revive them!"

Luna grabbed the vial out of Cullen's

pocket. She gave a drop to each Pikachu. Ash watched anxiously. The water worked quickly. First Pikachu's eyes sprang open. Then, Pikachu X sat up and blinked.

"*Pika!*" They were both fully revived.

"I knew the water was healthy," Luna said, "but its healing powers are absolutely amazing!"

"Stop muttering!" demanded Domino. "You can't stay here!" She pushed the prisoners along. Before long, they all found themselves in a prison cell.

"You better let us out of here!" shouted Ash.

But Domino was already walking away. She talked to Giovanni on her radio.

"Everything is going according to plan," she radioed. "Construction of our base is proceeding."

Outside the caves, huge cranes and other machinery were at work. Giovanni's new laboratory was taking over the island and destroying it. Hundreds of workers pounded away at the huge structure. They were making fast progress. But they were also dumping toxins and other pollutants into the waters.

"What's the status of Mewtwo?" asked Domino.

"Mewtwo is stronger than I realized," Giovanni barked. He could see Mewtwo struggling inside the pink orb. "If this goes on much longer its body will be destroyed before its will is."

"You can't destroy it! It could take years to clone it again!" Domino shouted.

"I know that," Giovanni hissed. "But this is a battle between Mewtwo's will and mine!" Giovanni clutched the radio with such frustration that it shattered.

Domino was frustrated, too. She yelled at two workers scrubbing the floor. "Can't you two work faster?"

Jessie and James looked up from the floor. They shot Domino a nasty look and went back to work.

On the other side of the island, the skies filled with thousands of Bug Pokémon. The swarms of Ledian, Butterfree, and Beedrill were so thick that their sound could be heard in the cave. The captured Pokémon became very excited. They cheered on the Bug Pokémon.

"What are they saying?" Ash asked Meowth.

"They say, 'They're comin' and they're very angry. The Bug Pokémon are mad at the people that are polluting the lake. They're coming to stop them!'"

Giovanni's Persian tried to warn him. But it was already too late. The Bug Pokémon crashed through his office window.

"What's happening?" Giovanni screamed. He was attacked by large groups of Beedrill. The Ledian and Butterfree went after the workers. They swooped down, terrorizing as they attacked.

The Butterfree attacked two workers who stood on a scaffold above a series of reactors. The workers held blowtorches that were ablaze.

"Hey . . . what's that . . ." the first man uttered. But he fell to the ground before he could say more. His blowtorch fell into the reactors.

In the prison cell, Ash and the others felt the ground shake.

"What's going on?" Ash shouted.

There was no time to answer. The entire island rocked with the explosion.

Chapter Ten

Rescue Mission

The island was still shaking when Brock pulled himself up from the ground.

"Look!" he shouted. The prison bars had been ripped away.

"A way out!" Ash cried. "Come on, everybody! Hurry!"

The prisoners rushed into the cave tunnels. They had to save Mewtwo.

Cullen turned to Luna. "I'm going back that way. I'm worried about the spring."

"I'll go with you," Luna agreed.

Outside the cave, the Bug Pokémon weren't finished. They destroyed the construction site and now they were after Domino. She fought back with her black tulip. But she was outnumbered. She turned to run.

"They'll never stop the Black Tulip," she crowed.

Just then, she hit the floor that Jessie and James had cleaned. It was slick with polish. As Jessie and James spied on her, Domino sailed across the floor and fell flat on her face.

"I guess that floor is still a little slippery," Jessie remarked. She and James laughed loud enough for Domino to hear.

By the time Ash, Misty, and Brock arrived at the orb, Mewtwo was very weak.

"*Pika-pi!*" cried the Pikachu clone.

"I am glad . . . you are safe." Mewtwo could barely get the words out. "I cannot bear this much longer." Its body was beginning to slump.

"Mewtwo," whispered Ash in awe.

"How do you know my name?" Mewtwo asked.

"We heard it from Meowth . . . and Meowth told us you're the one who saved my Pikachu. There's got to be some way we can help you now!"

"Stop these machines," Mewtwo uttered.

Brock searched for a cutoff switch. "It's no use," he said, "they're sealed up."

"We'll have to tackle them!" Ash declared. He hurled himself against the heavy metal machine. It didn't budge.

"Hit it harder!" Brock cried. He threw himself against the machine. Nothing helped. Meowth, Pikachu, and the clones joined in. No matter what they did, the machines wouldn't move. Finally, together they charged one of the machines. It rocked and fell to its side. But the electric bolt adjusted itself. It didn't break its connection. Mewtwo was still captive in the pink orb.

"We can't stop it," cried Brock.

"Then I must use what remains of my power," Mewtwo whispered.

The big Psychic Pokémon closed its eyes

and concentrated. The pain was terrible. Mewtwo shook violently.

Ash shouted to the two Pikachu, "Help out with your Thunderbolt!"

ZAP! The Pikachu hit the machines with two big electric shocks. In a last burst of painful energy, Mewtwo fought the evil energy. With the help of the Pikachu, the orb shattered. Mewtwo fell to earth in a heap.

"You did it," cheered Ash. "You beat him!"

"Yes," whispered Mewtwo. "But I have destroyed myself."

"*Pika-pika!*"

"The spring," cried Meowth, "they're saying, 'come to the spring, Mewtwo!'"

"Let's go," agreed Ash.

Giovanni had other plans. He and Domino appeared on the deck of his chopper. His army was behind him on the ground. "You're not going anywhere!" he bellowed. "Mewtwo belongs to me. I will decide whether it will survive or not."

"No, you won't!" shouted Misty. The Pokémon clones stood behind her. Onix,

Golbat, Geodude, and many others gathered to save Mewtwo.

"You take Mewtwo," Brock said to Ash.

Ash quickly put Mewtwo's arm around his shoulder and pulled him up.

"No!" shouted Giovanni. But Pokémon were everywhere. Gyarados and Dewgong exploded from under the water. The Beedrill, Ledian, and Butterfree swarmed above him. The other clones stood firm. Ash hurried away with Mewtwo.

"You wish to defy me as your leader has?" Giovanni barked at the clones. "Very well. I will crush you, too!"

One of a Kind

With Bulbasaur and Chikorita, Ash was able to get Mewtwo up to the spring.

"Why are you helping me?" Mewtwo whispered.

"You saved my Pikachu. That's a good reason," Ash answered. "Do you always need a reason to help somebody?"

"Perhaps you are a unique human," Mewtwo said. "One of a kind."

"You're one of a kind, too," Ash stated. "Everybody is."

Mewtwo laughed sadly. "I don't know what I am," he said.

"Ash!" Luna called as he approached the water's edge.

"This is Mewtwo," Ash told her urgently. "It's real weak and needs to get into that spring water fast."

Cullen stepped forward. "It might contaminate the whole spring! This water has minerals humans need!"

"I'm sorry but right now the one who needs that water most is Mewtwo," Ash replied. He gathered all his strength and threw the Pokémon into the water.

Mewtwo sank deep into the magical water. It felt the water begin to work right away. "I have seen this place. I have been here before. I feel new life rising within me," Mewtwo thought as it came back to life. "If these waters have the same restoring effect on me as they do on other Pokémon, could it be that this is my rightful place, too?"

Back on the lakeshore, Giovanni's choppers landed. "Tell me where Mewtwo is!" he roared.

"You cannot come here and destroy the spring!" shouted Cullen.

"Yes, I can," Giovanni replied. "This place belongs to me!"

But Giovanni was silenced. Mewtwo rose from the lake and soared into the sky. The Pokémon glowed with energy. "It does not belong to you," Mewtwo cried, "any more than I do! This place has given me new life. I shall use my power to defend it."

Mewtwo held out its arms. Its eyes began to beam. Columns of light flew across the sky. Then one huge beam of bright psychic energy came up from the lake, through Mewtwo and high into the sky. It was blinding and it shook the whole island.

When the beam disappeared, so had the lake and the clones — including Mewtwo. All that remained was dry bedrock. Giovanni stared at his army.

"What's happened?" Giovanni demanded. "Where is Mewtwo?"

Cullen and Luna knelt on the dark, dry earth. "The spring is gone." He held up the vial with the sample. "We may be able to create a synthetic version of the water in the lab."

"But what happened to the Pokémon?" Luna asked.

Ash and Pikachu were in awe. Misty giggled. Brock couldn't believe his eyes. Mewtwo had moved everything underground. The pure lake water now made sparkling pools in the bright, beautiful cave. Healthy, happy Pokémon were everywhere.

"This is amazing!" exclaimed Ash.

"I have moved the lake and spring beneath Mt. Quena to protect them," Mewtwo said.

"Wait until I call Professor Oak and tell him about this!" Ash said.

"You will tell no one," Mewtwo told him. "Once you leave this place, you must leave behind your memories of all you have seen here."

Meowth cried out, "You can't do that! It's only natural to wonder about who and where you came from and someday these little ones are gonna want some answers —

only there won't be any — not if you make everybody forget!"

Jessie and James were stunned. It was as if Meowth actually cared about the Pokémon.

"So what if their parents were clones, they're livin' creatures," Meowth continued. "They deserve to know about themselves just as much as anybody does!"

All the Pokémon nodded in agreement.

"*Meowth!*" said Meowth X.

"I think we should remember, too," added Ash.

Mewtwo thought for a moment. "Yes. They deserve to remember. I will clear only the memories of those who seek to destroy us."

As Mewtwo spoke, a flock of Butterfree flew over Giovanni and his army. They dropped a gentle mist on the evil crew. The air was filled with the sound of Butterfree as they flew off. Giovanni and Domino looked around. They were very confused.

"Double-oh-nine, why are we here?" Giovanni shouted.

"Maybe we're on some kind of secret mission?" Domino asked.

Giovanni was baffled. "We should withdraw our forces at once!" he commanded. Then, to himself he said, "It's strange. I have this feeling that I have been utterly defeated."

Across Time
and Space

Ash and his friends were already in their brand-new Pikachu-head balloon at the mouth of the cave. Next to them, Team Rocket was in their Meowth-head balloon. Mewtwo and the clones gathered around.

"Thank you," Mewtwo said gently. "I will always remember you."

"This time we'll both remember," Ash said and smiled.

Pikachu and Pikachu X said good-bye to each other. Then, Meowth turned to

Meowth X, "If you ever see our balloon, fly by and say hello!"

"*Meowth!*" Meowth X purred.

The balloons lifted off the ground and so did every kind of Pokémon. The sky was full of them and they all glowed.

Ash and Mewtwo looked at each other one last time. "If someday you hear my voice," Mewtwo said, "know that it is my spirit calling across time and space to yours."

The balloons flew high into the night sky. Ash watched the island disappear behind them. Then he looked ahead and wondered where his journey would take him next.

"I will remember you . . . always."

Ash jumped, startled by the voice.

"What's wrong, Ash," Misty asked.

"I could have sworn I just heard Mewtwo talking," he said.

"*Pika?*" asked Pikachu.

Ash smiled and said, "Maybe it was just my memory."